# The Magical Kingdom of Maralear

By Yvonne Ediger

Art By Madeline Clincke

Schreyer
Ink Publishing

The Magical Kingdom of Maralear
© 1997, Yvonne Ediger

Pictures © 2020, Madeline Clincke

Edited by Casia Schreyer

ISBN 978-1-988853-47-5

**WAITING...**

Bound with a silk ribbon, the old paper was stained, ripped, and wrinkled. It lay in the dark, waiting. It had been there a long time and could wait a long time more. A pair of matched rings were strung neatly on the bow, a part of the secrets the paper held.

It waited ...

# Chapter 1 – Katy and Becky

"Drop that princess you evil dragon! I will stab you with my sword. Ha!" Becky swung the broom handle in a wide sweep through the air. "Ha!" she cried again, stabbing the handle at her sister. Another wild sweep and – *smash* – all the toy ponies crashed to the floor.

"Becky! Stop throwing things around. Help me finish cleaning this stupid playhouse or I'll tell Mom," Katy said.

"I'm so bored of cleaning. I don't want to clean anymore. Let's find something else to do," Becky said.

"It's your fault we have to clean the playhouse. You're always whining, 'I'm bored, I'm bored'," Katy mimicked her sister. "Mom hates whining, and you should know by now that if you say you're bored, Mom will find you something to do, and me too. And it's usually cleaning."

Katy and Becky had moved to the country with their parents. No other kids lived close by so they only had each other to play with. They had things to do like playing in the old barn with the cats or jumping on the trampoline or playing in their playhouse, but still the first two weeks of summer vacation had been boring, boring.

Katy turned back to the pile of toys she was sorting. Becky stuck out her tongue and made a face at her sister. She made a couple of weak sweeps at the sand and dust on the floor. Her daydream played on in her head. She imagined she was a brave hero riding her unicorn to rescue the fair princess from the highest tower in the land.

She grabbed a doll from the floor and stuck her on the top shelf of the cupboard. There was an evil dragon flying in to frighten her! She picked up a pink dragon and swooped it around the playhouse before placing it on the shelf beside the doll. The broom became her sword again and she slashed it through the air. She poked the dragon and prepared to chop off his head with one mighty blow.

*Squeak!*

Becky's foot came down on a rubber ball. She lost her balance and – *crash!!* The broom smashed against the corner of the cupboard. The dragon fell to the floor with a clatter. The doll landed in the pile of ponies with a thump. And Becky landed in the middle of the toys Katy was sorting.

"BECKY!!!" Katy yelled. Her fists were held tight.

"I'm okay," Becky said.

"The cupboard isn't! Look what you did!" Katy pointed at the cupboard. The top shelf was missing a piece right at the corner.

Becky started to cry. She hated to be yelled at and if the cupboard was broken Katy wouldn't be the only one yelling.

"Okay, okay," Katy said. "I'm sorry I yelled at you."

Becky sniffled. "Maybe we can fix it." She picked up the piece of wood. She continued to sniffle as she tried to fit the piece back into the hole. It wouldn't go in no matter which way she turned it.

"Oh, let me do it," Katy said. She twisted the piece in her hand, studying the hole, trying to figure out which way it went. "Hey," she said. "There's something in here."

## Chapter 2 – The Map and the Magic

Katy reached into the hole and pulled out a rolled-up piece of paper. It was tied up with a faded blue ribbon. On the ribbon were two silver rings.

"Let me see," Becky said as she snatched the bundle away from Katy. Katy was quick. She grabbed the paper back again.

"Stop it," she said to Becky. She carefully held the roll of paper. "It looks old. See how yellow the paper is. It's all wrinkled and folded. And look at these rings. They might fit us. I'll untie the ribbon and we can each try one."

She tugged the ends and the ribbon slid open easily. The rings tumbled to the floor. The girls grabbed them and put them on. They fit perfectly.

"What's on the paper?" Becky asked as she admired the ring on her finger. It had a strange pattern weaving around it.

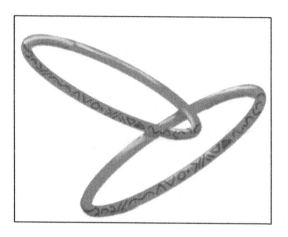

Katy looked at the paper. "It's a map," she said. "There's a poem here too." She read the poem aloud.

*In the magical kingdom I want to be*
*Oh grant this wish for me*
*Metal joined to flesh and bone*
*As I stand upon this stone*
*I wish to journey without leaving here*
*To the magical Kingdom of Maralear*

Becky shivered. "That's a weird poem. It sounds like a spell to make something magical happen."

"Look at this map," Katy held it out to Becky. "It looks like our yard and field. See how there's an 'X' marked here on the rock pile?"

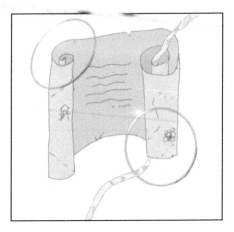

"Maybe it's a treasure map," Becky said. "Let's go to the rock pile. Maybe we'll find something."

"We won't find any treasure, Becky. We've been to the rock pile before."

"I know," Becky said. "But maybe we will." She jumped up and headed for the door. The sun was bright, and the wind was gently waving the branches of the nearby trees. Becky headed towards the field and the rock piles.

"Mom wants us to finish the playhouse today," Katy said, following after her sister. "Maybe we shouldn't go exploring right now."

"Mom won't mind if we take a short break," Becky answered.

"I guess not," Katy said. After a minute she said, "Knock, knock."

"No, Katy," Becky said. She hated knock-knock jokes.

"Oh, come one," pleaded Katy. "Knock, knock."

"Oh, all right. Who's there?" Becky replied.

"Boo!"

"Boo, who?"

"Don't cry, Becky!" Katy laughed. "Knock, knock."

"Nu-uh." Becky wasn't going to play anymore.

They arrived at the rock pile and climbed to the top. The rock pile was shaped like a doughnut, high around the edges and lower in the center, and was made of all the giant rocks the previous owner had pulled out of the field. They searched all around the pile for something to show where a treasure might be, but they found nothing.

Katy sat on her favourite rock, a sparkly pink and black one, and looked carefully at the paper. She turned it this way and that, trying to make it match exactly to the rock pile. When she thought she had it just right she tried to find where the 'X' might go. She decided on the large, flat, white rock but a closer look of the rock revealed nothing new.

"This is pretty stupid," she said. "I knew there wouldn't be any treasure. This summer has been so boring. I wish something magical would happen."

Katy sat on the rock with the strange paper dangling from her fingers. Becky sat nearby, daydreaming. The clouds overhead fascinated her. They always made her think of dragons and animals.

"This poem is pretty strange too, don't you think, Becky?" Katy went on as she glanced at the old, torn paper in her hand. She read the poem out loud once more.

*In the magical kingdom I want to be*
*Oh grant this wish for me*
*Metal joined to flesh and bone*
*As I stand upon this stone*
*I wish to journey without leaving here*
*To the magical Kingdom of Maralear*

Becky stared at her sister, her eyes and mouth wide. "Oh my," she stammered. "Oh, Katy. What is happening to you?"

## Chapter 3 – The Hole

Katy felt her stomach drop like when an elevator moves too fast. The world around her had completely changed. The rock pile was huge; it rose up around her like a mountain. Becky looked like a giant.

"Katy, you're so small!" Becky was amazed.

It was true. It wasn't Becky and the rocks that had grown, Katy had shrunk. She was now about the size of a cat.

Katy started to cry. "How did this happen? What am I going to do? I can't go back to school looking like this. Mom is going to freak out when she sees me."

Becky crawled over the rocks to Katy. She put her arm around her and tried to comfort her very tiny older sister. She started to cry too.

"I bet it was that weird poem," sobbed Katy. "We have to figure out how to make me the right size again."

"Maybe if you say the poem backwards it will work to make you grow," Becky said. She sniffled a bit.

Katy tried reading the poem backwards. Nothing happened. She tried reading the last line first and the first line last. Nothing happened. She stomped her feet and yelled, "I want to be big again!" Nothing happened. She sighed.

"Somehow we have to find a way to make you big again," Becky said. "Should I go and get Mom?"

"NO! She wouldn't believe this. What could she do, anyway?"

"I think you're right about this being a magic poem," Becky said.

Katy sniffled. She was scared she would never be big again. "The answer has to be here. This rock could be the magic stone in the poem. I didn't shrink when I read the poem in the playhouse. We will have to search for clues."

Becky took the tiny paper from Katy. It grew to normal size instantly. "We have to do it together." She read the poem.

*In the magical kingdom I want to be*
*Oh grant this wish for me*
*Metal joined to flesh and bone*
*As I stand upon this stone*
*I wish to journey without leaving here*
*To the magical Kingdom of Maralear*

She started to shrink right away. She climbed down the rocks to the ground in the center of the pile. Katy quickly followed her. They searched around the rocks hoping to find a clue to help them. Everything looked so different now and both girls were seeing things they'd never noticed before.

"Hey Katy look at this hole!"

Katy came down beside her. There, under a large rock, was a hole. A tunnel went downwards. A sign hung from the roof of the tunnel; it read 'Welcome'.

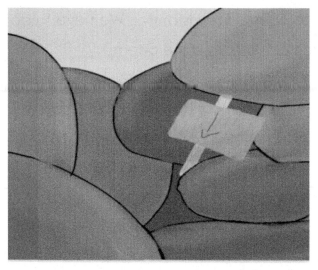

"That's amazing! I've never seen a hole here before."

"Should we go down?" Becky took a step closer without waiting for her sister's answer.

"Becky! No!" Katy screeched as she grabbed Becky's arm.

"But Katy, there's a light down there!" Becky had her head in the hole, and it muffled her voice a little. "I can see light, and something is down there. We should see what is down there. It may help us to grow big again."

Becky knew Katy wouldn't be able to resist now but still she held her breath and waited until Katy said, "Okay. Just a quick look."

They tried walking down the tunnel, but the slope was too steep. They lost their balance and tumbled down into a soft pile of dry grass. They'd fallen into a completely round room. The tunnel behind them went up and out. From the tunnel ahead came a softly glowing light.

"Hey Vinny, I think we've got company," A voice called out from somewhere ahead of them.

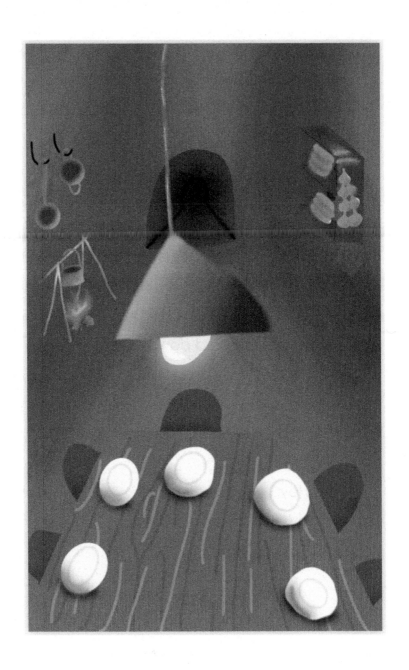

## Chapter 4 – Vinny and Maria

A little face peeked around the corner at them. Two pointy ears poked up from reddish fur. Two kind eyes shone black from the furry face. It was a fox.

"Hey, Maria, you're right! But you'll never guess who it is. It's the two young human girls," the fox said in surprise.

A second face peeked around the corner. It was smaller and whiter than the first but just as cute. "Oh my goodness! Well, come in, come in," she said to them.

Katy and Becky sat in the pile of soft grass. They couldn't believe their eyes or ears. There were two foxes inviting them in – it couldn't be real.

"We are just having dinner, but there's plenty. You're more than welcome," she beckoned to them with a dainty paw.

"What should we do?" Katy whispered.

"I guess we go in," said Becky. She swallowed the lump in her throat.

Katy and Becky cautiously went forward. Through the doorway they could see a cozy kitchen. "Sit, sit," Maria said. "Oh, my! Vinny, we are being rude to our new friends." She approached Katy. "I'm Maria Redfox, and this is Vinny, my mate."

"How do you do?" he responded and bowed to the girls.

"Hello," answered Becky. "We are, I mean, I'm Becky, and this is my sister, Katy."

"Hi," Katy said shyly. She held out her hand and Maria reached out her paw. Katy shook it gently.

"Dinner is ready," Maria said. "You really should join us. There's lots."

"Roast duck," Vinny said, setting the table. He licked his lips.

"Ok, we would like that very much," Katy said. She actually like things like roast duck. Becky was fussier, but she minded her manners and didn't say anything.

Katy and Becky settled at the table. They looked around as their hosts set the table and fetched the food. It was a large room, but cozy. The light came from a lantern over the table. A pot hung over a fire against one wall. Another pot and a frying pan hung on hooks nearby. There were dishes inside the cupboard. The walls were all rounded and they could see the packed earth. A second tunnel headed away from the one they had come down. There were no windows.

Vinny finished setting out seven bowls, leaving the girls to wonder – *why so many?* Next, he went to the second tunnel and gave a low whistle. Suddenly, the tunnel was filled with yipping and thumping. A flurry of furry bodies burst from the tunnel and tumbled into the kitchen.

23

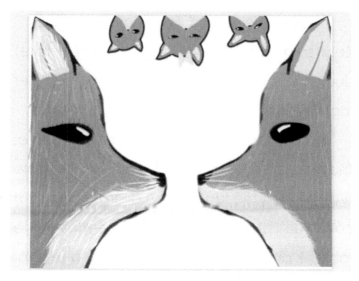

Three pairs of shiny little eyes peered curiously at the girls. The baby foxes were as adorable as kittens. They had pointy little ears and tiny paws. Their tails were long and fluffy. Each one was a different shade of red.

"Katy, Becky, meet our young – Zach, Melvin, and Dolly," Maria said proudly. The three little heads bobbed shyly at the girls. "Kits, we have guests. Katy and Becky live in the house past the trees, and they are joining us for dinner. Can you say hi?"

"Hi," chimed three little voices at one.

"Sit at the table kits, and let's eat," Vinny said. And they all did. Maria served up the duck while the kits looked shyly at the guests. They nudged each other and giggled at the girls.

## Chapter 5 – The Kingdom of the Field

"Maybe you can help us. How can we talk to you and understand you?" Katy said. "And do you know how we can get back to our normal size?"

"Well," Vinny started, "A few years back when we were raising our first littler of kits – "

"Zach, Melvin, and Dolly are our second litter born in this den," Maria explained. "The first litter has grown up and moved away."

Vinny nodded. "When we first arrived here, we heard stories. People who lived nearby had a way of shrinking down to the size of us animals, talking to us like we can talk to each other. The magic stone would allow them to enter our world if they knew the right words. They called the field The Kingdom of

Maralear. In Maralear, all the animals can talk to each other, and that must include people."

"Could they get bigger again when they left?" Katy asked.

"I think so. I had heard they came and went as they pleased. I don't know how they did it though," Vinny said.

"What other animals are living in this field?" Becky asked.

"Well, in Maralear there are a few others that I'm sure wouldn't mind meeting you. There are Kerri and Sanford the cranes near the swamp. And there is Airy and Free, they are hawks. They live in the trees near Kerri and Sanford."

"Don't forget Seymour," said Maria.

"He's smelly," said Dolly.

"Yeah, he's a skunk," said Zach.

"Wow!" Becky and Katy were amazed.

"There are also other animals, some who aren't very clever, and some who can be mean," Vinny said. "Rabbits are smart but they have a vicious temper, they like to kick and bite. The deer are all right but they are so big and kind of nervous. Mice and shrews are also very nervous. They are pretty smart but of course we don't talk to them because we eat them."

"You must be careful of the rats," Maria cut in. "They are always plotting some scheme or another."

"The ducks and geese," Vinny went on, "Have a very limited vocabulary."

"The say 'hi' to each other a lot," Melvin said.

"Is that what all the quacking is about?" Katy asked.

"Yes. That and 'run, run, run' and 'fly, fly, fly,' is about all they know," Vinny said.

Everyone giggled at the way he flapped his arms when she imitated a duck trying to fly.

As they were finishing their dinners, Vinny asked, "Would anyone like a quick game of 'Twist and Dodge' before I go on my afternoon hunting trip?"

"Yeah!" three little foxes yelled together.

"Would you like to play with us?" Zach asked the girls.

"How do you play?" Becky asked.

"We all stand on the top of the stones," said Dolly.

"And Dad yells out the directions," said Melvin.

"We have to move really quick," Dolly added.

"And if you fall, you're out," said Zach.

"Yeah," said Melvin.

Becky and Katy tried to follow but the kits spoke very quickly. Their heads and ears felt dizzy from the chatter.

"Maybe we could just watch?" Becky said.

"We should start looking for something to help us get big again," Katy said.

"It will be okay. We can play for a little while and then start looking," said Becky. "I think 'Twist and Dodge' sounds like fun."

"I've been thinking," said Maria. "Maybe Seymour can help you. He collects all kinds of junk and he's been here longer than most of the animals."

"When can we meet him?" Katy said. "How do we find him?"

"He's coming by later today," Vinny said.

"Then we have lots of time to play!" Becky said.

"Yeah!" the kits yelled. They hurried up the steep passage to the outside.

The girls followed the kits up the passage. It was easier going up the steep tunnel than it had been going down. The kits had all climbed to the top of the rock pile. They spread themselves along the top of the ring. There was room for Becky between Zach and Dolly. Katy climbed up beside Melvin. Vinny stayed at the bottom.

"Ready?" he called out.

"Ready!" replied all the kits.

"Maybe you two girls should sit down and watch for the first round," Vinny said.

Katy and Becky both sat down. They were tired from climbing up the passage and up the rock pile. The kits moved restlessly nearby. They were eager to get started.

"Left!" yelled Vinny.

The fox kits leapt left. They bounded from rock to rock, quickly and carefully.

"Right!" yelled Vinny. The kits made a quick turn and leapt to the right. "Up!" he yelled.

The foxes all quickly leapt high in the air. Dolly missed her footing on the way down and slipped on the rocks. She tumbled into the center, bumping rocks on the way down.

"I'm okay!" she called.

"Dolly's out!" Zach called back.

"Left! Right!" yelled Vinny.

Melvin missed the quick change in direction and ran straight into Katy.

"Oomff," Katy gasped.

"Melvin's out! I win, I win!" Zach danced at the top of the pile as he sang.

Vinny was proud of Zach. "Good for you," he said. "Shall we try again?"

"Yeah!" The kits loved this game. Dolly climbed back to the top. Becky and Katy were ready to try the game. They stood up.

"Right!" yelled Vinny.

Becky and Katy turned and began to move around the rock pile. It was easier, now that they were smaller, but the kits still moved much quicker.

"Up!" he yelled.

They jumped up as they had seen the kits do. Landing was not easy.

"Left!" Vinny yelled.

They quickly turned left. Melvin slipped and tumbled down into the centre of the rock pile. Falling didn't seem to bother the kits. "Down!" yelled Vinny.

Katy and Becky stopped. The kits quickly ran down into the centre. "Oh! That's what that means," Becky said as she laughed. She heard a whooshing noise. A huge bird swooped down and flew away with Becky.

## Chapter 6 – Up and Away

"Eeek!" screamed Becky. She could see the foxes and Katy getting smaller and smaller as she went up, up into the sky. She hung onto the sharp claw that was holding her. She didn't want to fall from way up here. "Help! Help!" she screamed as loud as she could.

"You sure are loud," said a voice above her.

"Help! Help!" Becky continued to scream. She could see the ground coming closer and closer as the bird started downwards.

What if the bird wants to eat me? she thought.

She screamed even louder. "HELP! HELP!"

THUMP. They landed. The bird continued to hold onto Becky. A second bird hopped closer.

"Hey, Airy, what's that?" asked the second bird.

"Don't know, Free. It was on the rock pile with the Redfox family. I thought it would make a tasty dessert."

"Let me have a look," Free said as he leaned down to peer at Becky.

Becky gasped. The hawk stared at her, turning his head back and forth. Becky put her hands over her eyes and held her breath.

"Well, I suppose it'll do, but I've never seen anything like it. Is it safe?"

"It sure was loud."

"I'm not sure that matters," Free said.

Becky decided she'd best try to get loose before she was eaten. "Let me go you mean old bird!" she yelled at Airy. "You shouldn't eat people you know."

Airy startled and jumped back.

Becky got to her feet. It was strange, being shorter than a hawk. "You're a bad bird!" She shook her fist at them.

"Well," said Free. "It's a human."

"What do I do with it?" Airy said.

"You can't eat it," said Free. "They're not usually so small though. Are you a runt?"

"NO! I've been shrunk by a magic spell." Becky was feeling a little safer now that the birds were talking to her instead of threatening to eat her. She rubbed her side where a claw had pinched her. She heard yipping coming towards them.

She saw Katy riding on Vinny's back. They were running through the grassy field towards them. It was the silliest thing Becky had ever seen, since Katy was nearly as big as Vinny.

"AIRY! FREE!" Vinny called from afar. "Don't eat that human!"

Vinny ran up to Becky, panting. Katy slid off his back. She grabbed Becky and hugged her. "Oh, I was so scared that bird would eat you before we got here," she said. "Are you okay?"

"Yeah, I'm okay," Becky answered. "I think I talked them out of eating me but if I ever have to ride with a hawk again, remind me to wear some padding. Those claws are sharp."

"Thank-you," said Airy, lifting his foot and flexing his claws proudly.

"I don't think she meant it as a compliment," said Free.

"Sounded like a compliment to me," said Airy.

"Maybe, the humans would like to see our new babies, to show that we're very sorry for the mix up," Free said.

Airy glanced at Becky and Katy, then Vinny. "They won't hurt our babies, will they, Vinny?"

"No," Vinny said. "I think they're okay. They seem like good folks."

"Okay," said Airy. He held out his foot. "Climb on. It's just a short ways up the tree." Becky sat on the hawk's foot and wrapped her arms around his leg. Katy did the same with Free and they were soon airborne.

Up in the tree was a neatly built nest with six off-white eggs. "They're just eggs," said Becky.

"Yes, but they will be birds very soon now," said Free.

"Don't foxes eat eggs?" asked Katy. "And don't hawks eat foxes?"

At the base of the tree, Vinny laughed. "I wouldn't eat my friends' eggs, and Airy and Free wouldn't eat their friends either. Humans eat eggs too, don't they?"

"Yes, they do," said Katy. "But I guess I wouldn't eat my friends' eggs either. Though I've never had a friend who lays eggs before."

"Yeah, it's kind of neat," said Becky.

"Well, we'd best get back to the rock pile. Maria will be worried about you, Becky, and Seymour should be arriving soon. We don't want to miss him. I'll give you two a ride back across the field."

The girls hopped a ride back to the ground with the hawks then climbed on Vinny's back.

"That's it," he said. "And we're off."

## Chapter 7 – Princess

Vinny trotted back towards the pile of rocks. The girls could see the whole field from atop Vinny's back. It stretched out in all directions. There were rock piles and small groves of trees scattered sparsely like islands around the field. A larger grove of trees could be seen in the distance. They could also see their dog, Princess, sniffing around the rock pile.

"Look Becky, there's Princess," Katy said, pointing.

Vinny stopped. "That dog has been hounding my family all summer. I'm afraid she'll catch one of our kits unaware one of these days. Do you know what kind of damage those teeth can do to an animal of my size?"

"Is it really that dangerous?" asked Becky.

"Yes. She could easily kill one of the kits," said Vinny. "If she were to catch me, I would put up a good fight, but I don't know if I would win. The best we can do is keep leading her away from the den."

"How ill we get back to the rock pile now?" asked Katy.

"What if we called her over here?" asked Becky. "Then you could get back to the rock pile and we could send her home!"

"What if she doesn't recognize us?" Katy asked. "She might think that we are mice or rats and try to eat us."

"If she can hear us then she would listen to us. Don't you think so?" Becky was sure their dog wouldn't hurt them. Katy wasn't so sure.

"I think we should be really careful about this. If she doesn't recognize us, she could really hurt us," said Katy.

"I know what to do," said Vinny. "There's an empty den over by that other rock pile." He pointed to their left. "If you go over there, you could hide in the den if anything goes wrong. Then I could come back and lure her away."

"Okay." The girls agreed to Vinny's plan.

Vinny ducked down in the grass staying out of sight. The girls hurried over to the second pile. They searched for the unused den. It wasn't hard to find. Once they were ready,

Becky stood at the top of the rock pile and waved to Vinny. Then she whistled for Princess. Katy stayed near the den waiting because she couldn't whistle.

Princess's ears perked up and she looked around the field. She headed towards the whistle at a gallop. As soon as it was clear, Vinny raced to his home. He quickly checked that his family was all right (they were fine, just worried about him and the girls). He climbed to the top of the rock pile and watched where the girls were in case they needed him.

When Becky saw Princess approaching, she climbed down to Katy and the two stood just inside the tunnel opening. They didn't have to wait long. Princess jumped to the top of the rock pile and started sniffing around. The girls could hear her muttering under her breath.

"Where are they? Where are they?" Her tongue hung out as she panted loudly. "Find them. Find them. Find them."

"Princess!" Becky called.

Princess spun towards the opening. "Fooled me. Bad mouse. Bad mouse," Princess muttered as she started digging. "Grrr. Bad mouse. Get mouse."

"Princess, go home!" Becky yelled at Princess. Katy grabbed Becky and dragged her further inside the den.

Princess heard her but went on muttering. "Bad mouse. Not fool Princess. Bad mouse." She continued digging and trying to get her head in the tunnel.

There was a swishing noise and Princess looked up. Airy and Free had seen the trouble the girls were having and had come to help. They swooped at Princess and glided back into the air. Princess snapped her teeth at them but they were too quick. They dive-bombed her again and again. Then Vinny was there. He let Princess see him and then took off for the far end of the field. Princess growled and leapt after him.

The birds settled on the ground near the tunnel. "Quick now girls," said Free. "Maybe we can fly you over to the den."

"That would be great," said Becky. Like before, the girls settled on the hawks' feet, holding tight to their legs.

"Will Vinny be okay?" Katy asked.

"You're such a worry wart, Katy," Becky said.

"He'll be fine," Free said. "He knows what he's doing." Next thing the girls knew they were in the air and rising fast.

"Wow! This is fabulous!" Becky yelled.

Katy opened her eyes. It was an amazing sight to see. The field was spread out below them like a painting. The air flowed past their faces in a gentle breeze, ruffling their hair.

In the distance they could see Vinny running ahead of Princess. He suddenly disappeared down another hole. They watched Princess lunge at the hole. They knew she must be snapping and digging in her effort to get at Vinny. Suddenly they heard a yelp and Princess turned and ran for home.

The birds circled down toward the foxes' den. The girls could feel that elevator feeling in their stomachs as the earth rushed up to meet them. They landed with a gentle bump. They thanked the hawks and quickly ran for the tunnel. Forgetting about the steep slope they wound up tumbling to the bottom again.

## Chapter 8 – The Rings

They had a happy reunion with the fox family. Everyone was yipping and talking at once. No one seemed worried about Vinny, so Katy stopped worrying too. Being with the foxes was fun. They were a happy bunch, but Katy was feeling gloomy. They were still no closer to solving their problem but at least they were safe for now.

Katy sat at the kitchen table thinking while Becky chatted happily to Maria and the kits. Katy thought about the poem and everything that had happened to them today. As she thought, she twisted the ring on her finger.

"I wonder if the rings have anything to do with the whole problem," she thought. She pulled off her ring. At the last second, she realized that if she grew, she would fill the fox den to overflowing. But when she tried to put it back on, the ring slipped and fell to the floor instead.

She didn't grow at all. The only thing that changed were the sounds around her. The happy voices changed to yips and barks. She stared at the foxes. Moments before she could understand every word they said and now it was like listening to – well – foxes. She ducked under the table and grabbed the ring, pulling it back on her finger. Instantly she could understand the words again.

"Becky," she exclaimed. "Try to take off your ring."

Becky was puzzled by Katy's outburst, but she did as Katy asked. Her ring slid off easily and Katy could tell by the look on Becky's face as she stared at the foxes that the ring did the same as hers. Becky slid her ring back on.

"It's nice to know that a piece of the puzzle is solved," Becky said.

Vinny popped into the kitchen. "I heard that. What's this about solving a puzzle?"

Katy explained how the rings allowed them to understand the animals' language.

Vinny did a little dance. "You see! One step closer. This is all going to work out, just you wait. We'll have you home in no time."

"How?" Katy said. She put the paper on the table. "We know the rings are magic, and they let us understand you. We know the poem is magic but it only works on the rock. But how do we reverse it? We've read this poem upside down and backwards and it didn't work!" She pushed the paper away.

Vinny picked it up. "You know girls, this paper looks like it was ripped in half."

"I bet the answer is there!" Becky said.

"Great, just great," Katy said. "We have no idea where the other half of that paper could be. For all we know Mom used threw it in the burn barrel."

"Oh Katy, it will be okay," Maria said.

She brought biscuits and some bowls of water to the table for everyone.

While they were nibbling on their snack, they heard a thump and a giggle from the tunnel.

"Vinny! Maria! I've done it again! This tunnel of yours is too steep. I hope you don't mind me just dropping in, but that nasty dog was after me again."

Everyone turned to the door as a skunk waddled in.

## Chapter 9 – Seymour

"Seymour!" Vinny jumped up and met Seymour at the door. "You know that you're always welcome here. Come and meet our new friends, Katy and Becky."

Seymour stopped short. His furry skunk chin dropped down in surprise and his eyes popped open wide. "Humans! I never thought I would ever get to meet a real live human and here's two. Wow! So pleased to meet you both." He hurried over and shook their hands. "My grandfather, Hector, told me tales of meeting humans. It was hard to believe all his stories. I can't believe it's true. How did you find the magic?"

"Actually, it was an accident," Becky said.

Katy nodded. "We found a map and a poem and some rings and here we are."

"But we don't know how to get back," Becky finished.

"Actually, Seymour," said Vinny. "We had hoped you could help us out."

"Me? I don't know any magic. What could I do?"

"I know you keep everything," Vinny said. "Maybe the answer is in that old junk pile of yours."

"It could be." Seymour slapped his knee. "Let's head over there and check it out." He headed back for the tunnel with Katy and Becky close behind.

As they passed through the small round room, Seymour chuckled again. "It's a good thing they leave that soft pile of grass there. Every time I come in this way – Boom! – down I go. Hee hee."

They stopped to wait for Vinny who was saying good-bye to Maria. "Be back soon," he said. Keep the kits inside a while. That dog is out again."

"Hurry up, Vinny," Seymour shouted. "We haven't got all day."

"I know, I know," Vinny said as he caught up with them. They climbed to the top of the rock pile and looked around.

"There's that stupid dog," said Seymour. "I wonder what she's chasing now."

"My mom always says Princess is a very smart dog," said Becky. "Why do you call her stupid?"

"All dogs are stupid," said Seymour. "They can't think for themselves, and they don't learn to speak properly. 'Sit', 'down', 'get', 'good', 'bad'. They follow orders just fine but that's all they know. Cats are smarter – they do what they want when they want, not just when someone tells them."

"That makes sense," Katy said. "When she was chasing us, she kept saying 'bad mouse,' and 'get mouse', she thought we were trying to fool her."

"Easily confused," Vinny said, nodding. "That's how we get away from her."

They were walking through the long grass, heading towards the far north end of the field. Vinny would peek over the grass tops every once in a while, to check where Princess was. They soon reached another rock pile. This one was different from the others. It was so old that the soil and grass had hidden all the rocks. It was higher than the others but still had that funny donut shape. Someone had used stones to build steps up to the top but thistles made it impossible to climb up.

"We don't need to climb up to get to my home," said Seymour. "Come around the back." They followed him around the hill.

Behind the hill was a grove of trees. They couldn't see into the grove because the trees grew thick and close. Vinny and Seymour herded the girls away from the trees and to a tunnel in the rocks.

This tunnel sloped downward in a gentle decline – nothing like the sudden drop of the fox den. They followed Seymour into a large room. It looked like someone was just moving in – or out. There were boxes of stuff piled all around and paper stacked haphazardly in leaning piles on top of the furniture. Bits of pictures and maps were tacked to the walls. Some of it looked like old magazines and newspapers while others looked like flattened chip backs and cracker boxes.

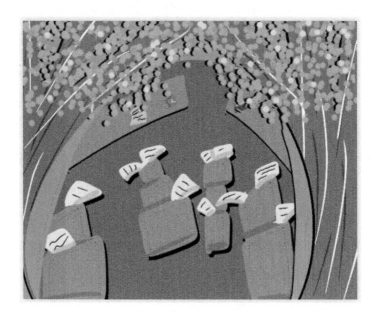

"Seymour!" Vinny sounded shocked. "I thought you were spending the summer cleaning this up!"

"Well, you know Vinny, it's so hard to do. I hate to throw away something important."

"Okay, okay. Let's get started on this mess of papers. We'll move fast. If anything looks like a map or a poem, we'll take a closer look."

Seymour gave each of them a box of papers to sort through. "These belonged to my grandpa, Hector. He kept every piece of paper he ever found. If there's an answer, it would be in his stuff."

Soon, Becky realized sorting papers was as bad as cleaning the playhouse. The musty smell was making her head hurt. She sat back and let her gaze wander around the room. Seymour seemed to be more of a packrat than a skunk. It was amazing what was in all these boxes, and all over the room. He'd hung the front of a salt and vinegar chip box on the wall, like it was a poster. And next to it was an actual poster of kittens in a basket – or at least a tattered piece of one. There was a scrap of map but Becky didn't recognize where it was from. Next to that ...

"Katy," she said, pointing at the wall. "There it is."

## Chapter 10 – Home

Hanging on the wall, between the kitten poster and a chocolate bar wrapper was a paper similar to the one in Katy's pocket. Seymour reached up to unpin it and handed it to Katy. Katy pulled out the first paper and laid the two side-by-side. There was the same map, and another poem.

"This looks right," Katy said. "But it looks like we have to take it to the rock before we read it."

Becky thought she'd feel excited when they finally found the answer, but she felt sad instead. She liked Vinny and Seymour and their other new friends and now it felt like the adventure was ending.

"I guess we should go to the rock and try out this new poem," said Katy. "It's getting late, and we should be able to get home now. Thanks for your help, Seymour."

"Anytime, anything," said Seymour. "Come back and visit again."

"Do you think we can really come back?" asked Becky.

"I'm sure of it," said Seymour. "My grandpa told me many stories of humans who visited him many years ago. I'm sure it's their magic you've found."

"Oh, that's great!" Becky said, dancing around the room. "Katy, isn't that great? We can come back whenever we want!"

"As long as we can get home again," Katy said.

"Well, Seymour, I should get these girls back. We'll see you soon."

They climbed out of Seymour's home and up on Vinny's back.

"It'll be quicker this way," Vinny said. "Hold on tight."

When they got back to the fox den, Maria and the kits came out to say goodbye.

"Will you come back to play soon?" asked Zach.

"Please," said Dolly. "We'll miss you."

"We'll try," said Becky, hugging them. "We've had so much fun today."

They climbed up the pile to the magic stone. Katy took the paper and read the second poem.

*Home is the place where I want to be*
*Oh grant this wish for me*
*Metal removed from flesh and bone*
*As I stand upon this stone*
*I wish to journey without leaving here*
*To leave the Kingdom of Maralear*

Katy waited but nothing happened. She was still small. She was afraid they would never get home.

"What did I do wrong?" she said. "I was sure it would work." She read the poem over again.

"Look," Becky said, pointing to the papers. "The first line of both poems tells you where you want to go. The second one is the same, it asks for a wish to be granted. The third line is weird. Metal, flesh, and bone. Katy! It's the ring!"

"I have mine right here," Katy said, waving her hand at Becky.

"Remember what happened when you took it off? Metal removed from flesh and bone. Maybe you have to take the ring off!"

Katy took her ring off. She tried reading the poem again. There was that dropping feeling in her stomach again. The baby foxes fled down the tunnel as Katy shot up to her normal size.

Becky tucked her ring in her pocket and read the poem. She shot up to normal size too.

They each bent down and patted Vinny and Maria as they said a last goodbye. They ran for home but stopped at the tree line between yard and field to wave at the foxes who sat and watched.

The girls knew the summer wouldn't be so boring now.

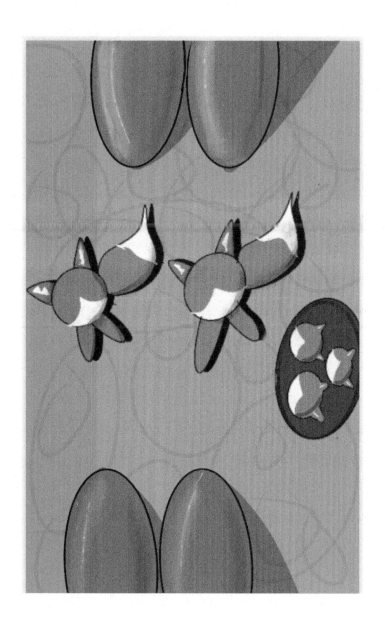

## Editor's Note

When I was in middle school my mom, Yvonne, took a class about writing books for kids. The Magical Kingdom of Maralear was one of the projects she did for that class. When it was completed, she sent it off to a few publishers, but nothing came of it. There was no self-publishing then, so she gave up on it, tossed the paper copy in a box, and we all forgot about it.

Years later, after my mother lost her battle with cancer, my dad found the old manuscript while cleaning out some boxes in the back of a closet. He passed it along to me, since I already had close to a dozen books self-published. The story was good, it just needed a little cleaning up.

I moved around some commas, cleaned up some run-on sentences, and added some details for clarity and ease of reading. All it needed after that were some black and white interior illustrations.

I'm not an artist by a long shot and my sister, who is an artist, was swamped with her own projects and her growing family. I mentioned this to my mom's brother, and he suggested asking his kids, my cousins. They were both exploring digital artforms.

His daughter, Maddie, was up to the challenge and soon I had colour cover and some beautiful interior artwork. Maybe it's not as polished or refined as a *professional* artist, but I thought it was wonderful and I knew my mom would love it.

I spent a few weeks retyping the document, doing the layout, and inserting all the pictures. And here it is.

Sadly, my mom never saw it finished, in print. And she never got to write the sequels she had planned.

My daughter is nine and she really enjoyed reading her Oma's book. I may ask her to help me continue the series like my mother always wanted to do.

I hope you enjoyed this labour of love. My mom deeply believed in the magic of reading, and I'm honoured to share her story with you.

## About the Author

Yvonne Ediger lived in Winnipeg, Manitoba with her husband and kids. When she wrote this book her daughters were in junior high.

Yvonne loved to read. She also enjoyed cooking, baking cookies, and knitting. Her favourite animal was a horse and when she was a teenager, she had a horse named Misty.

Yvonne lost her battle with cancer in 2012. She is deeply missed and fondly remembered.

**About the Editor**

Casia Schreyer is Yvonne's eldest daughter. She lives in rural Manitoba with her husband and two children. Casia has published over a dozen titles, including two picture books for children. She also edited Yvonne's memoir, a cookbook titled "Recipes and Memories".

Casia's hobbies include knitting, crochet, and woodworking.

## About the Artist

Maddie is Yvonne's niece. She lives in Regina, Saskatchewan with her parents and her brother. She loves dancing and art.

# Other Books from Schreyer Ink Publishing

Infant-9 years
Nelly Bean and the Kid Eating Garbage Can Monster - Casia Schreyer
Nelly Bean and the Adventures of Nibbles - Casia Schreyer
Janelle et le Poubelle

9-15 years
The Underground Series - Casia Schreyer
- Complex 48
- Separation
- Reunion
- Training
- Rebels
- Turncoats
- Sunlight
- Cheyanne and Other Tales from Underground
- Now Available in a single omnibus edition!

12 years – Adult
Recipes and Memories - Yvonne Ediger
The Ultimate World Building Book - Casia Schreyer
The Rose Garden Series - Casia Schreyer
- Rose in the Dark
- Rose from the Ash
- Rose without Thorns
- Rose Alone
- Rose at the End

Teen – Adult
Nothing Everything Nothing - Casia Schreyer
Pieces - Casia Schreyer
ReImagined - Casia Schreyer

Made in the USA
Middletown, DE
22 March 2022